For Eli and Sylvia—N.Z.J.

Anthony said, "Edward . . . you've got too much STUFF."

"How can anyone have too much STUFF?" answered Edward.

"What a bunch of junk," said Marguerite. "Get rid of it!"

"Junk! It's my STUFF! I can't get rid of my STUFF!" insisted Edward.

SNEAKERS AND FISH HEADS

And he didn't.
Edward continued to STUFF STUFF.

Soon there was no place for anything but STUFF.
Including Anthony or Marguerite.

Even the cat picked up and left.
The mice soon followed.

Edward hardly noticed.
He was too busy with his STUFF.

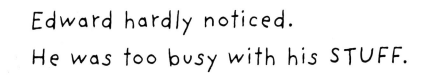

Anthony phoned Edward.
"Want to do something today?"

"Can't," answered Edward.
"Doing STUFF with my STUFF."

Marguerite stood by Edward's front door and shouted, "Come out of that STUFFY house!"

He didn't. Edward stayed STUFFED with his STUFF.

Then one day . . . A very large truck drove down Edward's street.

The rumbles were so big, they shook each and every house. Of course, that didn't matter much to the other houses. Only to Edward's.

(Which had all that STUFF.)

STUFF slid this way.

STUFF slipped that way.

STUFF teetered.
STUFF tottered.
And before Edward knew it . . .

No, the splat was *not* Edward.
Just some STUFF.

All that STUFF made a tiny empty
space surrounded by other STUFF with
only just enough room for . . . Edward!
"I'm saved! Saved by my STUFF!"
How good was that?
Well . . .

Not that good.
It got sort of boring stuck in there with
all his you-know-what.

Plenty boring.

Oh so boring.

In fact, Edward got plain old sick and tired of all that boring STUFF.

"I gotta get OUTTA HERE!"

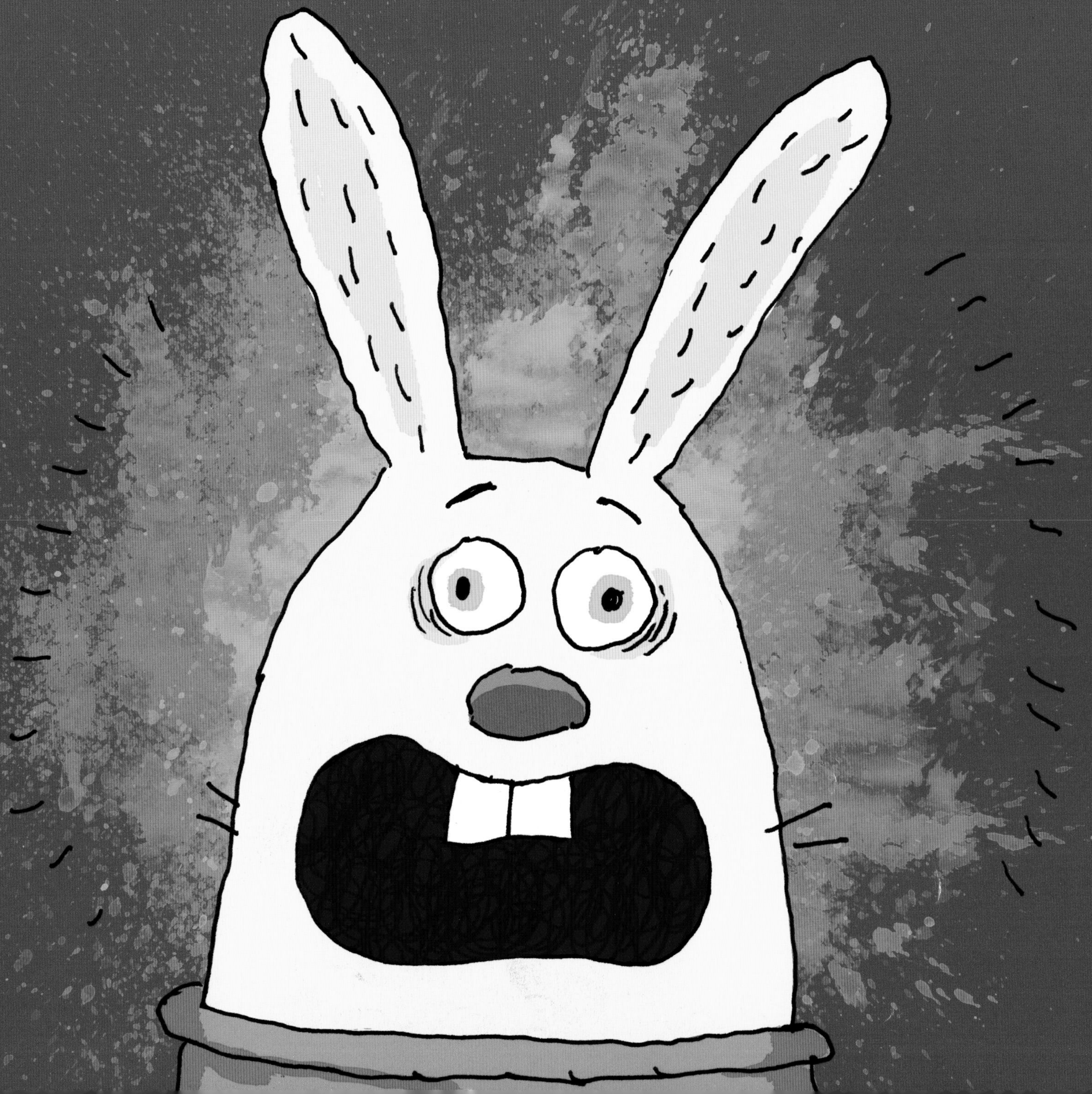

Truth be told, he missed Anthony and Marguerite.

Edward wondered what they were doing
while he was stuck with all his STUFF.

He shouted.　　He yelled.　　He whimpered.　　He whined.

No one heard him.
There was too much STUFF.

POOR EDWARD!

I HAVE A FEELING HE'll BE OKAY!

Then *many days later* . . .

Anthony and Marguerite came by the house and heard a soft, faint sound coming from way within.

"I think that is Edward!" said Anthony, ear to the door.

Marguerite agreed. "I would know that whiny whimper anywhere!"

The two opened the door—which was not easy!

They bravely burrowed, tunneled, and dug through STUFF. A LOT OF STUFF.

But they finally found Edward!

He was dazed, dizzy, plenty pale, and bored stiff from STUFF but was able to look at his friends and say . . .

"HELP ME GET RID OF THIS STUFF!"

Anthony and Marguerite were glad to do so.
They gave away STUFF to anyone and everyone
who wanted it or needed it, and sometimes they
just plain junked the junk.

PINBALL MONKEY

PINBALL MONKEY

FREE

IT'S ALL FREE

FREE

FREE

TURTLE SINGS THE HITS

SING!

FREE!

Which made a lot of people happy.

But most of all Edward, because now he had lots of room and loads of time—to do, well . . . Other STUFF.

He played games with Anthony.

He tangoed the night away with Marguerite.

Or he just hung out with his friends.

Which, as Edward discovered,
was really the best STUFF of all.

# STUFF

By Margie Palatini    Illustrated by Noah Z. Jones

KT KATHERINE TEGEN BOOKS
*An Imprint of HarperCollins Publishers*

Katherine Tegen Books is an
imprint of HarperCollins Publishers.

Stuff
Text copyright © 2011 by Margie Palatini
Illustrations copyright © 2011 by Noah Z. Jones
All rights reserved. Manufactured in China.

Library of Congress Cataloging-in-Publication Data
Palatini, Margie.
Stuff / by Margie Palatini ; illustrated by Noah Z. Jones. — 1st ed.
p. cm.
Summary: Edward cares more about his possessions than spending time with his friends, until
he becomes trapped in his house full of "stuff," hungry and bored.
ISBN 978-0-06-171921-9 (trade bdg.)    ISBN 978-0-06-171922-6 (lib. bdg.)
[1. Belongings, Personal—Fiction.  2. Friendship—Fiction.] I. Jones, Noah (Noah Z.), ill. II. Title.
PZ7.P1755 Su 2011    2009049900    [E]—dc22    CIP    AC

Typography by Rachel Zegar
11 12 13 14 15 SCP 10 9 8 7 6 5 4 3 2 1
❖
First Edition